Tales of a Severed Head

Tales of a Severed Head

RACHIDA MADANI

TRANSLATED BY MARILYN HACKER

YALE UNIVERSITY PRESS ■ NEW HAVEN & LONDON

A MARGELLOS
WORLD REPUBLIC OF LETTERS BOOK

The Margellos World Republic of Letters is dedicated to making literary works from around the globe available in English through translation. It brings to the English-speaking world the work of leading poets, novelists, essayists, philosophers, and playwrights from Europe, Latin America, Africa, Asia, and the Middle East to stimulate international discourse and creative exchange.

Published with assistance from the foundation established in memory of Calvin Chapin of the Class of 1788, Yale College.

Contes d'une tête tranchée originally published in 2005 by Éditions de la Différence, Paris.

Yale University Press books may be purchased in quantity for educational, business, or promotional use. For information, please e-mail sales.press@yale.edu (U.S. office) or sales@yaleup.co.uk (U.K. office).

Printed in the United States of America.

Library of Congress Cataloging-in-Publication Data
Madani, Rachida.
[Contes d'une tête tranchée. English & French]
Tales of a severed head / Rachida Madani ; translated by Marilyn Hacker. — 1st ed.
    p. cm. — (The Margellos World Republic of Letters)
Text is in English and French.
Poems.
ISBN 978-0-300-17628-5 (alk. paper)
I. Hacker, Marilyn, 1942 — II. Title.
PQ3989.3.M335C6613 2012
841'.92—dc23   2012007645

A catalogue record for this book is available from the British Library.
This paper meets the requirements of ANSI/NISO Z39.48-1992 (Permanence of Paper).

10 9 8 7 6 5 4 3 2 1

CONTENTS

PREFACE

Marilyn Hacker

*There is no danger greater for the State than
that of self-styled intellectuals. You would have
been better off remaining illiterate.*
—King Hassan II of Morocco

Rachida Madani, Moroccan activist, teacher, Muslim feminist, painter—and, preeminently, writer—was born in Tangiers in 1951, and still lives there. She writes that, an early reader, she had already envisioned being a writer at the age of six, "so that everything that passed through my mind wouldn't fall into oblivion." She read everything she could put her hands on, "from comic books to astronomy" to the French children's classics, and thus read all the works of the comtesse de Ségur before she was ten—a vision of an aristocratic, highly moralized European world of another century. She soon discovered poetry—the French Romantics first of all, whose work she tried to imitate at the age of twelve; then Baudelaire, Verlaine, Rimbaud, Lautréamont, and the Surrealists. Later came Sartre and Beckett's and Brecht's theater. She cites the Nouveau Roman in French, the books of Claude Simon, Marguerite Duras, and Michel Butor, as the literary current that impressed her most strongly in its re-vision of narrative. Although a seismic change was renewing Arabic poetry in the 1960s and 1970s, Madani knew her other mother tongue through its classics only, and through daily speech in an entirely other register.

Madani was a schoolgirl in 1963 when King Hassan II ascended to the throne and instituted a policy of repression of political opponents, both nationalist and Communist, targeting intellectuals—writers, poets, historians—in particular. "There is no danger greater for the State than that of self-styled intellectuals. You would have been better off remaining illiterate," the king proclaimed after a particularly brutal and bloody official response to a demonstration of workers, trade unionists, and students in 1965. He dissolved Parliament and assimilated its functions to the throne. The assassination of the exiled leftist leader Mehdi Ben Barka in Paris (with the collusion of the French police) followed several months later. This was the beginning of a period known to Moroccans as *les années de plomb* (the leaden years).

The repression was one reason for the emergence of a specifically Moroccan—and dissident—literature. New poets, fiction writers, and politically engaged songwriters and sociologists began to make their work public. Fatima Mernissi began to publish her groundbreaking semi-fictional, sometimes autobiographical studies of the lives of women in Morocco and in Islam. For the young Rachida Madani, it was the discovery of Francophone Maghrebin literature that gave her a focus for her own talent—the writing of the Algerian Kateb Yacine and the novelist Rachid Boudjedra—but especially her discovery of the specifically Moroccan magazine *Souffles* and the poets involved with it: the Surrealist Mohammed Khair-Eddine, who lived much of his short life in France, and the poet-activists Abdellatif Laâbi and Mostafa Nissabouri, all only a decade her seniors. The scholar Claude Reynaud has written that Moroccan poetry sprang from the contacts among Arabic, French, and Berber, and from reciprocal exchanges between orality and the written word—but, he adds, one could also say that contemporary Francophone Moroccan poetry was born under the influence of this youthful and comparatively short-lived journal.

Souffles was founded in 1966 by these poets, then in their twenties, who felt the urgent need for a poetic renewal in the Maghreb and a forum for it. In his editorial manifesto, Laâbi sought to differentiate this new writing from the work of writers complacent or collaborating with the regime, and from the earlier generation of Francophone Maghrebin writers, even including Kateb Yacine, who, he claimed, were writing primarily for a French readership while describing Maghrebin realities. Fairly quickly, a wider span of creative energy crystallized around the journal: that of filmmakers, painters, playwrights, critics, and theorists. While Moroccan in its inception, it was open to writers from the rest of the Maghreb, and to "Third World writers" working in or translated into French as well. *Souffles* was banned by the government in 1972. Abdellatif Laâbi, who was also the leader of a leftist student/worker group, was arrested that same year, at the age of twenty-nine, for his political activities and was to spend the next eight years in the notorious Kénitra prison. (In 2010, the Moroccan national library, in an agreement with Abdellatif Laâbi, put the contents of the journal online: an invaluable anthology of the early work of many important Francophone Maghrebin writers, it can now be consulted at http://bnm .bnrm.ma:86/ListeVol.aspx?IDC=3.)

Of the *Souffles* group, it was Mostafa Nissabouri (b. 1943 in Casablanca) who first befriended Rachida Madani, whose work most touched her, and who offered her commentaries and criticism of her own poetry: a mentor and a role model. Madani was a youthful militant who expressed her resistance with texts rather than participation in strikes or demonstrations. Among the arrested activists were young men and women who had been her classmates in high school or at university, natives of Tangiers like herself, whose families were close to hers. In a determined and increasingly politicized movement, the prisoners' families—notably their wives and mothers—demanded they be given increased access to books, to visits, and to trials, as most of them were being held without specific charge or sentence. (This decade and this movement are described vividly in Jocelyne Laâbi's memoir, *La liqueur d'aloès* [Aloe Brandy], published in 2005.) In the 1970s, Madani succeeded in sending her new poems to a militant prisoner friend, who, in turn, circulated them among the political prisoners, where they came to the attention of Abdellatif Laâbi. These were the poems that made up her first collection, *Femme je suis.*

Laâbi, from prison, encouraged her to publish, although this would have been impossible in Morocco at that point, especially as Madani wanted him to preface her work, despite the disastrous consequences this would have had in their home country. He arranged a long-distance introduction to a friend in France, Ghislain Ripault, a slightly younger poet and editor who had lived in Morocco and had published Laâbi's own early work in a series called Les Inéditions barbares. Ripault became the publisher of Madani's first book, prefaced by Laâbi, in 1981, a small edition with limited circulation.

Here is one of those poems, speaking directly to the situations from which emerged both the political rebels, and those who did not rebel:

I am there
in your cell
sitting in the corner
there for five years now, my old brother
                    pale and silent
                    I watch you
and they pass before my eyes
the hearses you could not follow.

There were thirty of us
in a history class
we were poets, artists
we were already men
        already women
and we had dreams

        for the men
        for the women
that's why, on the blackboard
we hung Mussolini
        Hitler
        Von Hindenburg
        and the old history teacher
and we would sing
we sang
we sang
        Victory.

They pass before my eyes
the hearses you could not follow.
Mimoun, the comedian
at term-end parties
became a cop
he salutes Mussolini
   salutes Hitler
   salutes Von Hindenburg
   and the old history teacher.
Don't cry, old brother
over the hearses you could not follow.

There are no longer thirty of us
Hazlim our poet
hurled his poor blind head into the fire
surrounds himself with little dogs and howls at humans
under the full moon
a huge song of love and
                      rancor.
Do not cry, old brother
over the hearses you could not follow.

There are no longer thirty of us
Fatima, tall bitter clown
wasn't beautiful, do you remember?
Her husband noticed this
then at the judge's feet
she killed herself
in a burst of laughter.
Do not weep, old brother
over the hearses you could not follow.

There are no longer thirty of us
The Other
our sister from the slums
our living water
the cool spring for our thirst
closed her long
black lashes on the world
dead of hunger in her cell.
Hold back your tears old brother
for that hearse you could not follow.

But we are many more
than thirty
and I am there
in your cell there,
sitting there in the corner
there for five years now,
                    old brother
pale and silent
you look at me
and in your eyes pass
people burning the hearses
          burning mussolini
                hitler

> von hindenburg
>   to make History over.

Madani began working on her second, organically unified book of poems a year or so later. While the poems of *Femme je suis* drew on the young poet's immediate experience, *Contes d'une tête tranchée* (Tales of a Severed Head) considers the issue of women's role in society, and the hierarchies oppressing both women and men, as she interrogates the frame of the thousand-year-old collection of tales (which may have migrated from Farsi into Arabic) that is *The Thousand and One Nights*—in which King Shehriyar, insanely distrustful of women, swears to marry a new wife each night and have her beheaded the next morning to prevent her from cuckolding him. In the story framing the tales, it is through the courage and wit of the young woman, Scheherazade, who volunteers to be the king's bride, and through the endless tales she invents and tells night after night (to her sister Dunyazad, in fact, with the king overhearing), that Shehriyar is healed of his obsession and the remaining virgins of his kingdom saved from death.

In *Contes d'une tête tranchée*, Rachida Madani's modern-day Scheherazade is also fighting for her own life and the lives of her fellow citizens. But in the twentieth and twenty-first centuries, and under the weight of Morocco's leaden years, the threat comes as much from dictatorship, official corruption, abuse and denial of human rights, poverty, and the detritus of colonialism as from the power still wielded over women by individual men. Madani's complex narrator, unlike Scheherazade, has no entry into the "palace." This is a story of contemporary resistance—but once again language provides the weapon. "I am no one / in Shehriyar's city," the poet says in canto XIX of the first tale: "I am nothing. / But I have words, / pauper's words / . . . stolen from the dogs' cemetery." The title of the book indicates ominously that a contemporary Scheherazade has less chance of prevailing than the original.

An American or European reader could, and not in error, interpret *Contes d'une tête tranchée* as being a feminist vindication—of political and social rights, of the right of the woman artist to recount and depict her story on her own terms. But the sixties, seventies, and eighties were in Morocco marked more deeply by severe political repression, and by the imprisonment and torture of dissenters, than by the identity-based liberation movements, feminist or ethnic, that the Maghreb nonetheless shared with Europe and both Americas. Madani's alternate Scheherazade is also the artist of any gender desperately trying to redefine her or his relationship with political power and those who hold it.

Rachida Madani writes that she first knew *The Thousand and One Nights* as a child, through stories told by her mother and older sisters, come to them through their grandmother, with no reference to their status as literature. The characters were as familiar as Cinderella or Puss in Boots for a European-American child (who would not necessarily think about Perrault or the brothers Grimm hearing these stories). *The Thousand and One Nights* resurfaced in a French translation when she was a university student, in the perhaps unlikely context of a class on the structure of the Nouveau Roman, with the "mise en abîme" of the *Nights*' tales posited as an insight into the experimental novelists' narrative strategy. In 1975 she read *La mille et deuxième nuit* (The Thousand and Second Night) of her friend and mentor Mostafa Nissabouri. His poems spin an entirely dystopic tale set in contemporary Casablanca. He is ruthless in stripping away Orientalist myth and cliché applied to and rallied against the Arab subject. Scheherazade herself, old and crippled, speaks in a different register, with no power to charm the harm from power. A decade later, the younger poet began her own sequence.

The figure of Scheherazade has elicited a varied and contentious response among contemporary Arab women writers. A 2004 anthology of Arab and Arab-American women's fiction, essays, and poetry is titled *Scheherazade's Legacy*, and there is at least one dissertation on Arab-American women writers' appropriation of the Scheherazade role or persona. However, the Tunisian writer and scholar Fawzia Zouari published an autobiographical/critical narrative, *Pour en finir avec Shérazade* (Getting Rid of Scheherazade), in 1996, in which the character becomes the avatar of the woman who speaks only to deflect attention from herself, her demands and needs: "Each time I was tempted to speak, Scheherazade came up with a new story which bade me keep silent." And in 2010, the flamboyant Lebanese poet and editor Joumana Haddad published *I Killed Scheherazade: Confessions of an Angry Arab Woman*—in English, quickly translated into both French and Arabic—another autobiographical manifesto of intellectual and sociosexual independence, of which Elfride Jelinek wrote: "Scheherazade has to die to be able to speak her true self, to tell her own story: that is, to become a human being." In contrast, the twelve-year-old niece of a Lebanese blogger asked her uncle: "Why would a woman like to kill Scheherazade? She told the story of Sinbad and she saved thousands of women who would have died if she were not a good storyteller. . . . I wish I had Scheherazade to keep me company."

I think it is at least partially the Orientalist baggage that has become associated with Scheherazade as an avatar of the (self-effacing, charming) Arab woman that accounts for these writers' rejections of a persona that could also be read as belonging to the long line of poet-trickster heroes, male and female, who wish precisely to deflect attention from themselves in order to get the best of the tyrant, the monster, or the enemy commander.

Rachida Madani as an Arab woman writer has at least as complex a relationship with the Scheherazade persona to symbolize the speaking subject as do these others. Her speaker makes frequent reference to Scheherazade but is a contemporary woman, or a composite of many women, in dialogue with her and with the frame story of the *Nights*, while commenting on and engaging urgent issues, and with no access to the tyrant's ear. There is often a male interlocutor, but he is not King Shehriyar:

> when the wisest one among you died.
> He would walk along filled with the cries of subterranean cities whose roofs he had torn off.
> He walked with his hand on her woman's shoulder,
> the man disfigured by his songs.

(The First Tale, XIV)

> *Here a black car waits for him.*
> *Here he was taken elsewhere*
> *where his fingers were cut off,*
> *where they blindfolded him*
> *and fired into his mouth*

(The Second Tale, VI)

Madani's narrator rejects but ultimately redeems the myth Scheherazade has become (that of the shamanic woman storyteller) by turning her own poetic attention—and the reader's—to the city-state surrounding the storyteller that, equally, generated her situation, ending the *huis clos* between storyteller and dictator. The image of a "palace rebellion" as an option is recurrent. She directs the reader's attention to the silenced poets of both sexes, a clear reference to Moroccan political prisoners and the poets among them. In the Second Tale, she introduces the heretofore inaudible voice of a mother addressing her daughter in the midst of violence. The poet also considers female physicality in youth and age, and the narrator's awareness thereof—in the third sequence, in particular—not an issue in the *Nights* (how could Scheherazade become middle-aged?).

> *Winters*
> *winters gathered around my wrinkles.*
> *Smoke fills my throat*

as I speak . . .
Is it the fire being lit even now
               in the crystal palaces?
Is it the fire flaming up even now
               among my listeners?
          (The Third Tale XV, ellipsis in original)

Also in the Third Tale, Madani calls up one trope of classical Arabic poetry: the desert evocative of loss and of a nostalgia that can be viewed with irony.

Abdellatif Laâbi was released from prison in 1980, and emigrated to France with his wife, Jocelyne, and their children in 1984. There was a general amnesty of political prisoners in 1999 preceding the death of Hassan II. *Contes d'une tête tranchée* was published in Morocco by Editions Al-forkane in 2001. A collection of Madani's poems, including this book, was published in Paris by Les Éditions de la Différence in 2006. It was followed by a prose narrative, *L'Histoire peut attendre* —which could be translated *History Can Wait* or *The Story Will Follow*—located between novel, memoir, and what the French call auto-fiction, that brings a woman traveler into dialogue with her dead sister and an enigmatic figure from pre-Islamic and Islamic tradition called al-Khadir (the Green Man). In the 1990s, the poet undertook a more thorough study of Islam while also devoting more time to painting: since 2009 her work has been exhibited in Morocco with enthusiastic reception. She is now working on a second novel and a new collection of poems.

The visceral passion and the generosity of scope of *Contes d'une tête tranchée* attracted me on first reading, along with its simultaneous distrust of and reexamination/reappropriation of multiple traditions. But most of all I wanted to transmit the energy, direct and lyrically accurate, of Madani's language, a French informed by disparate literary traditions and still entirely its own.

Tales of a Severed Head

PREMIER CONTE

I

Quelle ville et quelle nuit
comme il fait nuit sur la ville
quand une femme et une gare se disputent
une même moitié d'homme qui s'en va.
Il est jeune, beau
il s'en va pour un peu de pain blanc.
Elle est jeune, belle comme une grappe
              de printemps
qui essaie de fleurir une dernière fois
pour son homme qui s'en va.
Mais le train arrive
mais la branche casse
mais soudain il pleut dans la gare
                        en plein printemps.
Et il surgit de partout
il siffle puis traverse la femme
de toute sa longueur.
Où la femme saigne, il n'y aura plus jamais
                        de printemps.
La nuit, dans sa tête, sous l'oreiller
il passe des trains chargés d'hommes
              chargés de boue
et tous la traversent dans
                  toute sa longueur.
Combien d'hivers encore, combien de neiges
avant la première lettre qui saigne,
avant la première bouchée de pain blanc ?

FIRST TALE

I

What city and what night
since it's night in the city
when a woman and a train station argue over
the same half of a man who is leaving.
He is young, handsome
he is leaving for a piece of white bread.
She is young, beautiful as a springtime
                              cluster
trying to flower for the last time
for her man who is leaving.
But the train arrives
but the branch breaks
but suddenly it's raining in the station
                              in the midst of spring.
And the train emerges from all directions
it whistles and goes right through the woman
the whole length of her.
Where the woman bleeds, there will never be spring
                              again.
In the night, in her head, under the pillow
trains pass filled with men
          filled with mud
and they all go through her
                    the whole length of her.
How many winters will pass, how many snowfalls
before the first bleeding letter
before the first mouthful of white bread?

II

C'est peut-être la même ville
mais c'est une autre solitude
un autre chemin de pluie.
Un enfant marche dans la rue déserte
il suit un autre enfant
qui suit un chien
qui suit un autre chien
qui suit une odeur de pain.
Plus il s'approche de l'odeur
plus l'odeur de pain s'éloigne
voltige
      tournoie dans l'air
puis soudain monte se percher
sur le réverbère
         comme un papillon de nuit.
Et les deux petits garçons
et les deux petits chiens
au pied nu du réverbère
restent bouche ouverte
        dans un rond de lumière.
Et c'est la même nuit
et c'est la même solitude
et c'est le même enfant
dans la même rue
        dans la même ronde de réverbères.
Maintenant la faim sur sa joue
a rendu plus profond
le sillon tracé par les larmes.

II

Perhaps it's the same city
but a different solitude
another road of rain.
A child is walking down the empty street
he follows another child
who is following a dog
who follows another dog
who is following an odor of bread.
The closer he comes to the smell
the farther away the whiff of bread moves
flutters
      circles in the air
then suddenly climbs to perch
on the streetlight
          like a moth.
And the two little boys
and the two little dogs
at the bare foot of the streetlight
stay, open-mouthed
         in a circle of light.
And it's the same night
and it's the same solitude
and it's the same child
in the same street
        in the same circle of streetlights.
Now on his cheek hunger
has deepened
the furrow traced by tears.

Maintenant au bout de ses membres chétifs
il traîne un jouet de pauvre :
                              un carton
avec dedans un petit chien tout maigre
et une enfance toute rapiécée.

Cela fait un drôle de petit bruit
l'enfance rapiécée que l'on traîne
                              sur le pavé.
Mais l'enfant écoute la nuit
et rêve de toute sa faim
qu'il est devenu marin,
son carton un navire qui vogue
et porte loin son enfance
                    devenue oiseau
                              d'un seul tir d'aile.

Now with his scrawny limbs
he drags a pauper's toy:
                    a cardboard box
and in it a skinny little dog
and a patched-together childhood.

It makes a peculiar little noise
that patched-up childhood dragged
                    along the pavement.
But the child listens to the night
and dreams with all his hunger
that he has become a sailor,
his carton a ship which floats
carrying away his childhood
                    which becomes a bird
                        in one wing-beat.

III

Elle a perdu jusqu'à ses tatouages
la femme qui marche sur la falaise.
Elle a vendu ses bracelets
vendu sa chevelure
vendu ses seins blancs.
Elle a mis au clou sa dernière larme
sa dernière bouchée de pain.
Elle a parlé aux voisins
parlé au juge
parlé au vent.
Elle voulait son enfant la femme
qui marche sur la falaise.
Elle le voulait à elle
pour elle toute seule
l'enfant de ses entrailles.
Elle voulait le bercer encore
comme font toutes les femmes
doucement, doucement en chantant
comme toutes les nuits, le bercer
l'enfant de ses entrailles.

Mais les hommes
mais le vent la poussent sur la falaise.
Elle regarde l'océan
elle voudrait se précipiter dans l'océan
pour boire l'océan.
Mais d'un seul coup tous ses tatouages
reviennent s'installer à leur place

III

She has lost everything, even her tattoos,
the woman who walks on the cliff.
She has sold her bracelets
sold her hair
sold her white breasts.
She has pawned her last tear
her last mouthful of bread.
She has talked to the neighbors
talked to the judge
talked to the wind.
She wanted her child, that woman
who walks on the cliff.
She wanted him for herself
for herself alone
the child of her womb.
She wanted still to be rocking him
as all women do
gently, gently, singing
as she sang every night, to rock him
the child of her womb.

But men
but the wind push her out on the cliff.
She watches the ocean
she would like to hurl herself into the ocean
to drink up the ocean.
But suddenly all her tattoos
return to their places

et tous se mettent à parler en même temps…
D'un seul coup elle retrouve
les légendes vertes et bleues
inscrites dans sa chair.
Maintenant elle est debout face au ressac
ses yeux sont secs
sa bouche est un pli.
Maintenant elle quitte la falaise
et elle s'en va…
Maintenant, elle va vers sa propre justice.

and they all begin to speak at once . . .
All at once she finds
the green and blue legends
inscribed on her flesh.
Now she is standing facing the backwash
her eyes are dry
her mouth is a fold.
Now she leaves the cliff
and goes away . . .
Now she goes toward her own justice.

IV

Quelle femme et quel départ !

Elle a nommé sa peur
elle lui a mesuré les pieds
puis elle a mesuré sa propre bouche
puis elle s'est élevée d'un pas.
Elle fait le tour de la cité de verre
fait du porte à porte
elle parle
et rien ne peut plus l'arrêter.

Elle parle de toutes les nuits
et de toutes les femmes
elle parle de la mer
des vagues qui emportent tout
comme si tout était à emporter,
des vagues qui recommencent la mer
là où elle s'est arrêtée.
Elle fait le tour de la ville
elle marche avec la mort
la main dans la main
et sa main ne tremble pas...

Elle parle autour de votre crâne
et quel rire dans sa gorge, cette femme
si au pied du mur, Shahrayar, surgissait !

IV

What a woman, what a departure!
She has named her fear
she has measured its feet
then she measured her own mouth
then rose up in one movement.
She goes through the glass city
goes from door to door
she speaks
and now nothing can stop her.

She speaks of all nights
and all women
she speaks of the sea
of waves which carry everything away
as if everything could be carried away
of waves which begin the sea again
there where the sea stopped.
She goes through the city
she walks with death
hand in hand
and her hand does not tremble . . .

She speaks all around your skull
and what a laugh would burst from her throat, that woman,
if, at the wall's base, Shehriyar arose!

V

De combien de villes châtrées
la femme est-elle née ?
De combien d'hommes-vampires
de demi-dieux ivres de sables ?
Combien a-t-il fallu de pommes
pour dégringoler du ciel ?
La terre est si peu vaste
qu'elle va toujours vers le même arbre
est-ce toujours la femme qui va vers l'arbre ?
Je me contenterai d'une grenade
et jamais je ne me sentirai coupable
d'être cette pomme qui te tranche
> *la gorge*
car je ne suis pas née de ta lèvre
je ne suis pas née de ton cœur
ni de ton crâne
et si j'avais su que tu resterais
> *tordu à vie*
je ne serais pas née non plus
> *de ta côte.*
Combien a-t-il fallu de pommes
pour que tu dégringoles nu du ciel,
demi-dieu ivre de sable ?

V

Of how many castrated cities
is the woman born?
Of how many vampire-men
and demi-gods drunk on sand?
How many apples had
to tumble down from the sky?
The earth is so far from vast
that she always goes toward the same tree
is it always the woman who goes toward the tree?
I would be satisfied with a pomegranate
and I would never feel guilty
of being that apple which cuts
                          your throat
because I was not born from your lips
I was not born from your heart
or your skull
and had I known that you would stay
                          crooked for life
I would not have been born
                          from your rib either.
How many apples did it take
to make you tumble naked from the sky
demi-god drunk on sand?

VI

De quelle ville châtrée
la femme est-elle née ?
Pourquoi une seule rue
et si étroite ?
Pourquoi s'en va-t-elle coupée en deux
ses mains précédant son corps ?
Pourquoi s'en va-t-elle faire le tour
                        de votre crâne
la femme qui a épuisé ses larmes ?
Combien de portes fermées vous séparent ?
Combien de mots lancés contre votre porte
avant que vous ne sortiez sur la place ?

VI

Of what castrated city
is the woman born?
Why only one street
and that one so narrow?
Why does she leave cut in two
her hands preceding her body?
Why does she leave to go around

                           your skull

the woman who used up her tears?
How many closed doors separate you?
How many words hurled against your door
before you come out on the square?

VII

Cette femme qui marche à l'horizon
qui marche depuis toujours
qui marche depuis qu'elle n'a plus de jambes pour marcher
Cette femme sans sourire, sans regrets
sans illusions en marche vers sa parcelle d'azur,
sait-elle que le temps n'est plus à la halte ?
Que le temps n'est plus au pardon ?
N'est plus à l'attente devant l'arbre
qui ni ne se meurt ni ne vit ?
Sait-elle la femme en marche vers sa parcelle d'azur
que le ciel a changé de goût
que le ciel est noir et que l'océan
l'océan clair et riant de son enfance
en frémissant monte et redescend
le long des vaincues ?

VII

That woman who walks on the horizon
who has always been walking
who has been walking since she no longer had legs to walk
    with
That woman with no smile and no regrets
no illusions, walking toward her plot of blue sky
does she know that time is no longer at her stopping point?
That time is no longer there to grant forgiveness?
Is no longer waiting in front of the tree
which neither lives nor dies?
Does she know, that woman walking toward her plot of blue
    sky,
that the taste of the sky has changed
that the sky is black and that the ocean
the bright and joyous ocean of her childhood
rises and falls trembling
alongside the defeated women?

VIII

Elle a brûlé ses terres avant de partir
elle a incendié la plus haute tour
                              de votre ville
car elle ne croit pas à ces voix blanches
                              dans vos livres
ni à ce coq haut perché qui prétend à lui seul
lever une nouvelle aube.
Elle ne croit pas à cette paix qui la passe
sous le pressoir de votre silence
ni à vos soirées dansantes au profit des dormeurs
à la belle étoile.
« Je te donnerai l'adresse de mon coiffeur
et ma plus belle recette de crabes. »
Paix en pâte d'amandes
et danse
danse jusqu'aux transes
dans les bras des nouveaux marabouts-guérisseurs
qui t'exorcisent
reprennent ton corps et recommencent
selon les caprices de la richesse
et de l'esprit.
Paix, paix sur leur corps que préservent
les amulettes modernes des comptes bancaires.
Paix sur elles qui connaissent
                              les paroles à dire
et les paroles à taire autour d'un banquet
où tout est dit sur
                              le chemin à suivre.

VIII

She burned her fields before leaving
she burned the highest tower
                              of your city
because she doesn't believe in those white voices
                                        in your books
nor in that cock perched high above who thinks he alone
can make a new dawn rise.
She does not believe in that peace which pushes her
into the winepress of your silence
nor in your parties at the expense
of those sleeping outdoors:
"I'll give you my hairdresser's address
and my best recipe for crab."
Marzipan peace
and dancing
dancing into a trance
in the arms of new marabout-healers
who exorcise you
take your body back and start again
according to the whims of wealth
and wit.
Peace, peace be with their bodies preserved by
the modern amulets of bank accounts.
Peace be with those women who know
                              the words to say
and the words to be silenced at a banquet
where everything is said about
                              what road to take.

Paix de petits fours et thé à la menthe
avec juste ce qu'il faut de maquillage
                            autour de l'œil
pour ne pas voir ses rides.
Jamais vous n'affaiblirez la tempête
qui gonfle sa poitrine vers les places publiques
où le vent cogne votre tête
et vous fait saigner du nez sur les murs.
Elle a brûlé la plus haute tour de votre ville
où vos palabres verdissent
                            en toute conscience
le long des murs.
Elle a brûlé vos villes avant de partir
un seul mot lui reste à dire
après mille et une nuits pour
                            sauver sa peau,
un seul mot
après mille et une nuits en pure perte.

Peace of petits fours and mint tea
with just the right amount of makeup

        around the eyes

to hide her wrinkles.
You will never undermine the storm
that swells her chest toward town squares
where the wind slams your head
and makes your nose bleed on the walls.
She has burned the highest tower of your city
where your chatter comes into leaf

        shamelessly

along the walls.
She burned your cities before leaving
she has only one word left to say
after a thousand and one nights to

        save her own skin,

only one word
after a thousand and one nights of pure loss.

IX

Je est le mot unique à proclamer.
Je dis Je
et j'ai l'air d'être moi
mais le Je est innombrable
dans la fièvre de ma poitrine
dans le désastre de ma poitrine.
Je est innombrable dans le jardin de verre
où pend, douloureuse des branches,
toute une forêt d'arbres
vers le bassin où s'étiolent
de pauvres esclaves aux noms de bijoux.

Sous l'œil torve d'une armée d'eunuques
suis-je revenue dans ce vacarme de rapaces ?
Est-ce le jardin d'autrefois
le même hibou hululant ma mort ?
ou est-ce moi réapparue dans ce même cauchemar
sous une épaisseur de moisissures ?
Suis-je jamais partie de ce jardin
                              aux portes closes ?
Ai-je vraiment pu un jour tromper la vigilance
du Grand Vizir, chef des eunuques
et coupeur de têtes dans ses moments de loisirs ?

Est-ce moi cette femme prisonnière de Shahrayar ?
Est-ce moi cette femme qui tresse sa chevelure
tresse sa rancune
et le chemin d'où nul ne reviendra ?

IX

I *is the word, the only one to be pronounced.*
I say I
and I look like myself
but the I *is innumerable*
in the fever of my chest
in the catastrophe of my chest.
I *is innumerable in the glass garden*
where hangs, with sorrowful branches,
a whole forest of trees
toward the pool where they wither,
poor slaves with jeweled names.

Beneath the vicious eyes of a eunuch army
have I returned to this racket of raptors?
Is this the long-ago garden
the same owl hooting my death?
or have I reappeared in the same nightmare
beneath a layer of mold?
Did I ever leave this garden
                         with locked doors?
Was I really able, one day, to escape the vigilance
of the Grand Vizier, head of the eunuchs
and headsman in his off moments?

Am I this woman prisoner of Shehriyar?
Am I this woman who braids her hair
braids her grudges
and the path from which no one returns?

Est-ce à moi cette voix plus légère qu'une plume
mais écharde
mais émeute
dans le harem de Shahrayar ?
Suis-je revenue sur mes pas dans ce palais de cristal
où je suis seule avec toi, ô ma chevelure
le seul cri ?
Où suis-je ?
Qui suis-je ?
Pourrait-on un jour se poser d'autres
                                        questions ?

Is it mine, this voice lighter than a feather
but still splinter
still riot
in Shehriyar's harem?
Have I retraced my steps back to this crystal palace
where I am alone with you, O my long hair,
the only cry?
Where am I?
Who am I?
One day can we ask ourselves different
                                        questions?

X

Il est vrai que pendant des siècles
elle a donné du front dans des villes absurdes
pour se constituer un squelette
à sa mesure.
Un vrai squelette de femme, tendu

               comme une harpe
et sonore dans ses moindres recoins.
Un rêve étranglé parmi tant d'autres
pour que soit payé en sang et en

               larmes,
son tribut à Shahrayar.
Il fallait jouer cloué dans la cité

               de Shahrayar,
reclouée sous les pas d'un être invisible
entre ciel et terre,
le jeu sans fin des palais sans portes
des rideaux tirés à la hâte
et des couvertures de soie

               sur couvertures d'émeraudes.

X

It is true that for centuries
she has gone head-on against absurd cities
to make herself a skeleton
to measure.
A real woman's skeleton, taut

     as a harp

and resounding in its smallest crannies.
A strangled dream among so many others
for which a tribute will be paid in blood

     and tears

to Shehriyar.
She had to play locked in Shehriyar's

     stronghold,

nailed down again beneath the steps of an invisible being
between sky and earth,
the unending game of doorless palaces
of hastily drawn curtains
and silken coverlets

    on coverlets of emerald.

XI

Je n'ai jamais quitté l'enceinte de ce jardin
jamais été au-delà de ses murailles.

Depuis des siècles que je suis à la recherche
d'une brèche où souffler dans ce château de cartes,
jamais pu franchir la rangée d'esclaves
à la solde de Shahrayar.

Nouée moi à ce jardin par des milliers de lianes
par le parfum vénéneux de vos belles phrases
plus que par mes actes.

Mes actes ne comptent pas
je n'y suis que par l'absence de mes désirs.

Je n'est d'ailleurs pas.

Je est immobile.

Ne pas bouger est l'ordre suprême,
mais bouger pour courir vers quelle brèche ?

Je est bâillonné.

Se taire
ne parler que sur ordre de Shahrayar,
mais a-t-on déjà vu une femme se taire ?

XI

I have never left the enclosure of this garden
never been beyond its walls.
For centuries I have been searching
for a gap to breathe through in this castle of cards,
I have never been able to break through the ranks of slaves
                              in Shehriyar's service.
I am tied in this garden by thousands of vines
by the venomous perfume of lovely sentences
more than by my actions.
My actions do not count
I take part in them only by the absence of my desires.
Besides, there is no I.
I *is immobilized.*
Not to move is the supreme command,
but move to run toward what gap?
I *is gagged.*
To fall silent
only speak on Shehriyar's orders,
but have you ever seen a woman stop talking?

XII

Je dis Je
et ma haine éclate dans le jardin de verre.
Ici la transparence n'est pas pour voir
                                            plus clair
n'est pas pour voir plus loin.
Ici la clarté sert à mieux éblouir
le regard pénétrant que vous pensiez avoir,
sert à nous rendre visibles
au troisième œil de Shahrayar
                                      votre maître...
Inutile de creuser les murailles
vous êtes visibles, entendez-vous ?
Visibles
et de toute façon morts.
Inutile de fuir
hommes si peu désireux de vivre,
tous ces yeux alignés sur vos fronts
ressemblent fort à des trous de
                                      balles.

XII

I say I
and my hatred bursts in this glass garden.
Here, transparency is not for seeing
                              more clearly
is not for seeing farther.
Here, clarity is used to further dazzle
the penetrating gaze you thought you had,
is used to make us visible
to the third eye of Shehriyar

                              your master . . .
Useless to dig into the walls
you are visible, do you understand?
Visible
and in any case, dead.
Useless to flee
you men who care so little for your lives,
all these eyes lined up on your foreheads
strongly resemble
                              bullet holes.

XIII

Son âme arrachée au-dessus de la falaise
comme l'aigle le plus féroce plane
et plonge dans l'écume.
De tout le poids de son désir l'océan s'élance
vers la femme qu'ils lui ont reprise.
Plus d'un est venu à son secours
plus d'un a réchauffé son encre :
« Relève-toi, crache cette eau amère.
Je suis là et puis l'amour
égaux nous deux en amour
tu feras la morte entre mes bras si tu veux,
si tu veux nous nous aimerons dans l'aride
comme Qaïs, comme Leïla
et puis fou de toi
fou d'être moi
je m'abattrai sur le sable
brûlé d'amour, Moi
le fou de moi-même
et de Leïla... »

XIII

Her soul snatched up above the cliff
as the fiercest eagle soars
and plunges in the foam.
With all the weight of its desire, the ocean rushes
toward the woman they had taken back from it.
More than one came to her rescue
more than one warmed up his ink:
"Arise, spit out that bitter water.
I am here and then love
the two of us equal in love
you can play dead in my arms if you like,
if you like we will love each other in barrenness
like Qaïs, like Leïla
and then mad about you
mad from being myself
I will fall down on the sand
burnt with love, I
my own fool
and Leïla's . . ."

XIV

Elle a brûlé ses terres
lorsque le plus sage d'entre vous est mort.
Il marchait plein de cris de villes souterraines
dont il avait arraché les toits.
Il marchait sa main sur son épaule de femme,
l'homme défiguré par ses chants.
Elle n'avait rien
                  plus rien dans ses paumes,
il avait quelques miettes de poèmes
dans un mouchoir sanglant.
Ils marchaient hachés par le vent,
il n'y avait rien d'autre à faire
contre cette boule le long de la nuque.
Un seau qui monte et descend au fond
                    d'une pierre
rien à tirer de la pierre.
L'angoisse engendrait l'angoisse
le long des murs où ils marchaient.
Les murs engendraient la soif
qui engendrait le tempête
en chants de guerre portant haut
                  l'étendard des errants.

XIV

She burned her fields
when the wisest one among you died.
He would walk along filled with the cries from subterranean
    cities
whose roofs he had torn off.
He walked with his hand on her woman's shoulder,
the man disfigured by his songs.
She had nothing
              nothing left in her hands,
he had a few crumbs of poems
in a bloody handkerchief.
They walked ripped by the wind.
There was nothing else to do
against that lump along the nape.
A bucket which rises and drops to the bottom
                    of a stone
nothing to be drawn from the stone.
Anguish begot anguish
along the walls where they walked.
The walls begot thirst
which begot a storm
of war songs hoisting
             the banner of wanderers.

XV

Il chantait le poète
si près de son cœur de femme
mais quand elle eut supplié :
« Vers quel visage moi
                qui ne suis pas encore ?
Vers quelle oasis moi
                parmi les vivants ? »
il creusa un puits pour cacher
                    ce qu'il écrit,
puis soudain blanc, soudain fantôme
il fondit dans le désert où se calcinent
                        toutes les lèvres
où s'effritent tous les désirs,
et se prenant pour Ducasse
            il s'effaça la bouche.

XV

He sang, the poet,
so close to her woman's heart
but when she pleaded with him:
"Toward what face do I go
                who still am not?
Toward what oasis do I go
                among the living?"
he dug a well to hide
                what he wrote,
then suddenly white, suddenly a phantom,
he melted in the desert where all lips
                        are burnt to cinders
where all desires crumble away,
and taking himself for Lautréamont
                        he erased his mouth.

XVI

Cet homme que la mort tient
à bout de bras
avec des pinces,
quel ver le mangera ?
Et si la terre se mettait à fuir
                    autour de son corps ?
Si son cercueil se lézardait ?
Si ce mort refaisait surface
comme un poisson pourri ?
Si le cimetière ramassait son linceul
et fuyait en se bouchant le nez ?
Où iraient respirer les morts
                    si tous les vivants
                            puaient ainsi ?

XVI

That man whom death holds
at arm's length
with tongs,
what worm will eat him?
And if the earth decided to flee
                    from around his body?
If his coffin cracked?
If this corpse floated to the surface
like a rotten fish?
If the cemetery gathered up his shroud
and fled holding its nose?
Where will the dead go to breathe
                    if the all living
                              stink like this?

XVII

Mais vous allez tous pieds nus
ou vous êtes tous assis sous le même
                              figuier stérile ;
Vous regardez votre tête posée à vos pieds
trop lourde pour vos oreilles
votre main la tâte et ne la reconnaît plus.
Votre crâne s'en ira sans votre corps
vos jambes ne le suivront pas
ni vos mains trop nues
ni votre cœur trop froid.
Votre crâne suivra sans vous son chemin
                              d'interrogations.
L'homme n'est pas toujours digne
                              de sa tête
vous le savez, frères décapités.

Un homme qui ne s'est pas assis
un homme qui ne sait pas s'asseoir aux
pieds de ceux qui se tiennent debout,
un homme qui a su garder toute sa tête
                              bien à lui,
un homme sous le figuier stérile a parlé.
Il a dit l'azur
il a dit la mer
il a dit tous dans la même barque
                              vers la même rive
et l'homme est mort
                    foudroyé
                              sous le figuier stérile.

XVII

But you all go barefoot
or you all are sitting under the same
                        barren fig tree;
You look at your head placed at your feet
too heavy for your ears
your hand gropes it and doesn't recognize it.
Your skull will go off without your body
your legs won't follow it
nor your too naked hands
nor your too cold heart.
Your skull, without you, will follow its road
                              of questions.
Man is not always worthy
               of his head
you know this, decapitated brothers.

A man who is not seated
a man who does not know how to take a seat at
the feet of those who remain standing,
a man who knew how to keep his head
                     to himself,
a man beneath the barren fig tree spoke.
He said the blue sky
he said the sea
he said all in the same boat
               toward the same shore
and the man died
          struck down
               beneath the barren fig tree.

XVIII

Un autre s'est levé
et chaque fois ses mots injustes
lancés en boules puantes dans ce livre
                                        qu'il écrit.
Dans quelle boue de ce pays lointain a-t-il
                                enterré ses mains ?
Et s'il traîne sa tête comme on traîne
                                ses savates,
comment peut-il se croire encore poète ?

Ouvrez son livre et vous entendrez
un cri de mort
et vous la verrez nue
et vous la verrez sale
et vous la verrez courir vers la mer,
se laver des mots
pour briller à nouveau
                        de tout son azur.
Vous avez beau secouer son livre
il y a longtemps qu'il est vide
comme si tous les mots s'étaient donnés
la main pour en fuir...
Il y a longtemps qu'il s'est donné la mort
après avoir mangé toutes ses femmes
et s'être déclaré l'Ogre
le plus grand
le plus beau
l'Unique ogre de toutes les légendes
pour enfants débiles.

XVIII

Another man arose
and each time his unjust words
hurled in stinking gobbets in that book
                                he writes.
In what mud of that far-off country has he
                            buried his hands?
And if he drags his head as someone might drag
                                    his slippers,
how can he think that he is still a poet?

Open his book and you will hear
a death cry
and you will see her naked
and you will see her filthy
and you will see her run toward the sea,
to wash herself clean of words
to shine once more
                    with all her azure.
You will shake his book in vain
it has been empty for a long time
as if all the words took each other's hands to flee . . .
He killed himself a long time ago
after devouring all his wives
and declaring himself the Ogre
the biggest
the handsomest
the Only ogre in all the tales
for stupid children.

XIX

Je ne savais même pas lire
dans la nuit qui a déchiré mes mains.
Je ne suis personne
            dans la cité de Shahrayar
je ne suis rien.
Mais j'ai des mots,
des mots de pauvres,
                déchirés de toutes parts,
des mots volés dans le cimetière des chiens
au nez des esclaves.

Et c'est avec ces mots que je projetais
de miner le palais de Shahrayar,
de faire crisser le jardin de verre
sous les dents de Shahrayar.
Mais quand j'ai voulu parler, ils m'ont dit :
« Tais-toi
et sois belle pour lui.
Tais-toi, nous parlerons à ta place,
nous te raconterons dans tes voyages
                dans tes déchirements,
nous te thématiserons
nous te prendrons en charge
                pour la postérité. »

Ils disent Elle
et j'ai l'air d'être moi.

XIX

I didn't even know how to read
in the night that ripped my hands.
I am no one
      in Shehriyar's city
I am nothing.
But I have words,
paupers' words,
      tattered all over,
words stolen from the dogs' cemetery
from beneath the slaves' noses.

And it is with these words that I intended
to erode Shehriyar's palace,
to make the glass garden screech
under Shehriyar's teeth.
But when I wished to speak, they said to me,
"Be quiet
and be beautiful for him.
Be quiet, we will speak in your place,
we will recount you in your wanderings
      in your rendings
we will make a theme of you
we will take charge of you
      for posterity."

They say She
and I seem to be myself.

Mais Shahrazade n'est qu'une invention
                              d'hommes
pour réhabiliter Shahrayar.
Shahrazade n'est que partie remise
                        dans le massacre.
Et c'est ansi qu'on a volé mes phrases
dénaturé mes phrases,
ainsi mis dans la bouche
                      mille et un contes
dont je ne savais encore rien.
C'est ainsi que ses chiens
m'ont rendue encore plus prisonnière
                        de ses casbahs,
encore plus fantôme
moi qui voulais être sans fin.

Je ne savais même pas lire
dans la nuit qui a déchiré mes mains
tandis que lui
ni homme ni femme
savait même écrire
parlait en mon nom
me volait ma bouche
                      ma seule arme
dans la cité de cristal.
Tandis que l'autre drapé dans ses silences
ponctuait son rire
m'offrait nue
            aux yeux des esclaves.

But Scheherazade is only an invention
                    of men
to clear Shehriyar's name.
Scheherazade is only revenge postponed
                    during the massacre.
And it's thus that they stole my sentences
distorted my sentences,
thus put into my mouth
                    a thousand and one stories
of which I still knew nothing.
It's thus that his dogs
made me even more of a prisoner
                    in his casbahs
still more of a ghost
I who wished to be endless.

I didn't even know how to read
in the night that ripped my hands
while he
neither man nor woman
even knew how to write
spoke in my name
stole my mouth
          my only weapon
in the city of crystal.
While the other draped in his silences
punctuated his laughter
offered me naked
          to the eyes of his slaves.

Elle a brûlé ses terres
lorsque le plus sage d'entre vous est mort
plein d'encre sur les doigts.

She burned her fields
when the wisest one among you died
with ink-stained fingers.

XX

Les Grandes Gueules au rire savant
ont retroussé leurs poumons
et moi j'ai mesuré le bras
où pendait le fou de Leïla.
Les voici ces muscles délivrés de

leur amour

les voici cercles tournant
dans le vide de vos orbites.
Voici les os de ma main
et me voici moi qui écris
œil pour œil

dent pour dent.

Mais que vous dirai-je moi ?
Que vous dirai-je entre les lignes
que vous n'ayez déjà su
déjà tu
déjà ravalé, ô Grandes Gueules
horloges parlantes

à la foire

des mots ?

XX

The Loudmouths with their knowing laughs
have rolled up their lungs,
and as for me, I've measured the arm
where Leïla's madman hung.
Here they are, those muscles, delivered
                                        of their love
here they are, turning circles
in the void of your eye sockets.
Here are the bones of my hand
and here am I who write
an eye for an eye
            and a tooth for a tooth.

But what will I say to you about myself?
What to tell you between the lines
that you had not already known
already silenced
already peeled back, O Loudmouths
talking clocks
        at the fair
            of words?

XXI

« Bah, cédons-leur la place
laissons-les s'exprimer
           s'expliquer
à coups de perles rares.
À tes mots
homme friand de larves,
à ta plume fétu de paille
et sors-nous encore de tes eaux noires
quelque huître hermétique
interprétable et fécondable
              à merci.

Mais ne viens pas nous défendre
ne viens pas nous consoler
ne viens pas nous chanter la tendresse
            des sirènes mutilées
les bras déployés en épouvantail.
Tu n'as rien proclamé
rien aboli
999 pages n'ont rien atténué
derrière les sept portes de l'enfer
à peine t'y ont-elles aménagé une place.

Mais il est vrai que nul noyé
n'est allé plus loin que le fond de mer,
nul pendu ne s'est balancé
plus haut que son abre. »

XXI

"Bah, make room for them
let them express themselves
        explain themselves
by means of rare pearls.
By your words,
man with a taste for maggots,
by your pen, a wisp of straw
and once more out of your black waters pull up for us
some hermetic oyster
interpretable and fecund
                as you like.

But don't come to defend us
don't come to console us
don't come to sing to us of the tenderness
                        of mutilated mermaids
their arms stretched out as scarecrows.
You have proclaimed nothing
and abolished nothing
999 pages have made nothing easier
behind the seven gates of hell
they have barely gained you a place there.

But it is true that no drowned man
has gone farther than the seafloor,
no hanged man has swung
up higher than his tree."

Ainsi par sa bouche
dans le jardin de verre
parla toute une nuit la chouette
                    la plus noire.

Thus all night long
in the glass garden
spoke through her mouth
                    the blackest owl.

XXII

Sept sentinelles
sept portes ouvrant sur sept labyrinthes
sept cents miroirs facettes de femme
et toi...

> *enfermée dans ton velours*
> *enfermée dans ton écrin*

à palabrer pendant mille et une nuits,
à bercer Shahrayar,
ô Shahrazade,

> *Shahrazade, où sont les actes ?*

XXII

Seven sentinels
seven doors opening on seven labyrinths
seven hundred faceted mirrors turned on women
and you . . .
>   *imprisoned in your velvet*
>   *imprisoned in your jewel box*
to chatter for a thousand and one nights,
to cradle Shehriyar,
O Scheherazade,
>   *Scheherazade, where are your deeds ?*

XXIII

Où je marche je vois des portes
et ce n'est pas plus clair
et ce n'est pas plus simple.
Où je marche je vois des femmes
et les femmes se tordent le long
                              des branches.
Un mur à gauche, un mur à droite
et de la mousse partout pour qu'il fasse
                              plus noir.

Verrai-je la fontaine où l'eau devient ébène
devient barque, devient rame
                              et se précipite ?
Verrai-je la fontaine qui devient plume
devient aigle,
                    devient espace ?
Verrai-je les hommes sur leur monture
se ruer vers le sommet de la montagne
d'où l'eau chute
                    dans l'eau qui fait voir
où je vois une île
                    où je marche
                    où tous les hommes et toutes les femmes
                    ensemble
                              rament vers les astres ?

XXIII

Wherever I walk I see doors
and it's not clear
and it's not simple.
Wherever I walk I see women
and the women twist themselves
                    along branches.
A wall to the left, a wall to the right
and moss everywhere, to make it
                    even darker.

Will I see the fountain where the water becomes ebony
becomes boat, becomes oar
                    and hurls itself?
Will I see the fountain which becomes feather,
becomes eagle,
          becomes space?
Will I see mounted men
gallop toward the mountaintop
from where water gushes
                    into the water that lets us see
where I see an island
                    where I walk
                    where all the men and all the women
                    together
                         row toward the stars?

XXIV

Tournant dans des couloirs souterrains
toujours devancée par ses cris
et toujours muette ;
Cherchant cette femme à voir
et tournant jusqu'à perdre la vue ;
Tournant et cherchant, cette femme, une brèche
dans ce palais enfoui sous terre,
une blessure dans le marbre
par où fuir et remonter
vers les racines des arbres,
fuir et remonter, serpent fébrile,
vers la porte
       à l'entrée de la mer.

XXIV

Turning along underground corridors
always preceded by her cries
and always mute;
Seeking a glimpse, that woman,
and turning till she can no longer see;
Turning and seeking, that woman, a gap
in that palace buried in earth,
a wound in the marble
through which to flee and ascend
toward the tree roots,
flee and ascend, feverish serpent,
toward the door
       that leads to the sea.

XXV

Je dis Je
et des bras multiples se précipitent
autour de mon cou frêle.
Je
devient le chiot qu'on noie.
Mais il n'est pas dit que je serai seule
à mourir
ni que je mourrai avant toi.
Il n'est pas dit que je mourrai
sans prendre les armes.

Tu es le maître
notre maître tant que tu détiendras
la clé des petites portes
      pour publier un livre...
Mais il n'est pas dit que je mourrai
sans prendre les armes :
Nous sommes liés
    par notre sang
        toujours versé
par quoi d'autre peut-on être liés
toi et moi
dans la cité de Shahrayar ?
Il suffit que je dise Je
pour que ma haine éclate dans le jardin
        de verre,
qu'un escalier m'aspire vers une porte
secrète, hors de la chambre royale.

XXV

I say I
and innumerable arms rush
to seize my fragile neck.
I
become the puppy that they drown.
But it is not written that I will be the only one
to die
nor that I will die before you.
It is not written that I will die
without having armed myself.

You are the master
our master as long as you hold
the key to the little doors
                    to publishing a book . . .
But it is not written that I will die
without having armed myself:
We are linked
            by our blood
                    always spilled,
whatever else could link us
you and I
in Shehriyar's fortress?
I need only say I
and my hatred will burst in the glass
                            garden,
and a staircase will draw me toward a secret
door, out of the royal bedroom.

Une porte interdite parmi toutes
où des chevaux ailés attendent
                              le grand départ.

Je partirai pour mieux revenir
dans ta cité de verre.
Tu es le maître
mais que devient un maître
dans une mutinerie d'esclaves ?

A door forbidden among all doors
where winged horses await
            the grand departure.

I will leave, all the better to return
to the city of glass.
You are the master
but what becomes of a master
when the slaves rebel?

DEUXIÈME CONTE

I

L'oreille qui m'entend
sait-elle qu'elle doit se pencher
                         sur ma bouche ?
Que le temps est aux chuchotements
qu'elle est sourde
et qu'elle m'entend,
que ma bouche forme son cri ?
Sait-elle l'oreille qui m'entend
que toutes les bouches sont fermées
sur le même cri ?
Sait-elle que ma bouche chuchote
quand toutes les fontaines se sont tues ?
Saurait-elle pousser son murmure d'eau
la bouche ouverte qui m'entend ?
Saurait-elle avec moi former mon cri
qui remplit sa poitrine
et remplit ma bouche
la bouche ouverte qui m'entend ?

SECOND TALE

I

The ear that hears me
does it know it must bend
$\qquad$*over my mouth?*
That this is a time for whispering
that it is deaf
but it hears me,
that my mouth forms its cry?
Does it know, the ear that hears me
that all mouths close
on the same cry?
Does it know my mouth whispers
when all the fountains have fallen silent?
Will it be able to utter its watery murmur
the open mouth which hears me?
Will it be able to join me to create this cry
which fills its chest
and fills my mouth
the open mouth that hears me?

II

Je ne peux marcher indéfiniment
dans la nuit
sans me demander pour quand l'aube
qui me délivrera de la nuit
> *où j'avance.*

Je ne peux me résoudre à siffloter
> *dans la nuit*

pour dorloter ma peur
ni ne peux me résoudre à trouver cette peur
obligatoire sur le chemin
> *où je vais.*

Je déchirerai le marbre
j'ouvrirai la porte des harems
je soulèverai la trappe des
> *cités souterraines*

et mes pas au soleil me seront comptés
pour être sortie indemne des contes de Shahrazade
indemne et lucide pour perpétuer le cri
> *de toutes les tombes*

car j'ai écouté aux tombes
comme on écoute aux portes fermées.
Ah, si je savais par quelle voie détourner
toutes ces oreilles d'eunuques
je raconterais votre mort
jusqu'à retourner tous les vivants
dans leur tombe...

II

I can't walk through the night
forever
without asking myself when a dawn will come
that will deliver me from the night
I move through.
I can't resign myself to whistling
in the night
to cosset my own fear
nor can I reconcile myself to finding fear
obligatory on the road
I'm traveling.
I will rip apart the marble
I will open the harem gates
I will lift the trapdoors of
underground cities
and my footsteps in the sun will be numbered
for having escaped unscathed from Scheherazade's tales
unscathed and clearheaded to pass on the cries
from all the tombs
for I have listened at graves
the way one listens at closed doors.
Oh, if I only knew how to divert
all those eunuchs' ears
I would tell your death
until the living turned over in their graves . . .

C'est parce que le sable et la peur
se mêlent dans la même voix qui parle
que cette femme continue de ramper
                                    vers vous
de vous chercher dans votre sommeil
comme si elle connaissait tous les raccourcis
qui mènent à votre bouche...

Qui avance ?
Vers quelle nouvelle peur ?
Qui prétend sauver qui ?
Qui pourra jamais vous sauver
hommes mutilés,
gardiens de la chambre royale,
si la nuit ne monte à votre gorge ?

Et c'est ainsi que j'avance
                ligne après ligne
sans illusion aucune
et c'est ainsi que le sable me prend
et que je vois rouge la mer
qui vers moi s'avance.
Mais je déchirerai le marbre
mais j'ouvrirai la porte des harems
mais je soulèverai la trappe des cités souterraines
même si mes pas au soleil me sont comptés.

It's because sand and fear
are mixed in the same speaking voice
that this woman continues to crawl
                              toward you
to search for you in your sleep
as if she knew all the shortcuts
that lead to your mouth . . .

Who moves forward?
Toward what new fear?
Who claims to save whom?
Who could ever save you
mutilated men, guardians of the royal chamber,
unless night rises in your throats?

And it's thus I move forward
                    line after line
with no illusions
and it's thus that the sand overcomes me
and I see the reddening sea
advance toward me.
But I will rip apart the marble
but I will open the harem gates
but I will lift the trapdoors of underground cities
even if my steps in the sunlight are numbered.

III

Elle avance à contre-courant
les veines ouvertes
elle avance à flots.
De métamorphose en métamorphose
de poème en poème elle avance
et chaque poème est une barque
vers l'autre rive.

Donne-moi ta main, ma rose
la rivière reste à traverser
dans toute l'ampleur de sa vase
qui sait combien de naufrages encore
avant l'aube ?
Donne-moi ta main
doucement je chanterai
doucement pour toi dans le noir
et ma voix onde dans la nuit
jusqu'à l'autre rive portera
les papillons frêles de ton rire.

III

She moves upstream against the current
her veins open
she moves in torrents.
From metamorphosis to metamorphosis
from poem to poem she moves forward
and every poem is a skiff
headed for the other shore.

Give me your hand, my rose,
the stream is still there to be crossed
all its depths of sludge
who knows how many more shipwrecks
before dawn?
Give me your hand
I'll sing softly
softly for you in the dark
and my voice a wave in the night
will carry to the other shore
the frail butterflies of your dream.

IV

Elle chante pour son enfant
comme si une chanson pouvait
                              préserver son rire
pour que le rire soit la chanson suprême
après la nuit la plus noire.
Comme si elle pouvait déposer dehors
                              toutes ses larmes
et rentrer sécher son linge.
Elle chante comme si tous les hommes
étaient derrière elle
et toutes les femmes en place,
comme si la peur n'était pas ce fleuve
qui traverse la ville en long et en large
comme si la peur n'était pas le refrain
                              unique de la chanson.

IV

She sings for her child
as if a song could
        preserve her laugh
so that laughter would be the final song
after the blackest night.
As if she could put all her tears
                outdoors
and go back in to dry her laundry.
She sings as if all men
were behind her
and all women in their places,
as if fear were not that river
which crosses the city's length and width
as if fear were not the song's
        one refrain.

V

Mais prends garde aux chansons
où la mer est absente
car quelle musique ma rose
si la tempête ne t'agite ?
Je chante afin qu'éclate le marbre
qu'éclate le cristal et tous les palais
où je fus esclave soumise
ou concubine royale,
ainsi ma mort sera la chanson dernière
après toutes les morts.

Mais chante pour moi
quand je m'abattrai
sur l'autre rive.

V

But beware of songs
in which the sea is absent,
for what music my rose
if the storm does not shake you?
I sing so that marble will shatter
so that all crystal and palaces shatter
where I was once a dutiful slave
or royal concubine,
thus my death will be the last song
after all those deaths.

> *And sing for me*
> *when I fall*
> *on the other shore.*

VI

Chaque poème est une barque
vers l'autre rive.
Ici le vent agite sa tête jaune
                    de pleureuse païenne
et les hommes tombent des branches
comme fruits pourris.
Ici les maisons se penchent de toutes
                    leurs fenêtres
et s'écrasent dans les rues.
Ici les poètes meurent en prison.
Ici une voiture noire l'attend.
Ici on l'a emmené ailleurs
où on lui a coupé les doigts
où on lui a bandé les yeux
et tiré dans la bouche.
Ici, juste là
on n'a pas pu l'enterrer.

Je te sauverai des villes
comme je t'ai arrachée aux sables
ma rose habillée de vents et de pluies,
nous deux dans la barque
et mon sang fou d'esclave rebelle hurlant
hurlant jusqu'à l'autre rive.

VI

Each poem is a skiff
headed for the other shore.
Here the wind shakes its yellow head
                                of a pagan mourner
and men fall from the branches
like rotten fruit.
Here houses bend from all
                          their windows
and crash into the street.
Here the poets die in prison.
Here a black car waits for him.
Here he was taken elsewhere
where his fingers were cut off,
where they blindfolded him
and fired into his mouth.
Here, just over there,
they could not bury him.

I will rescue you from the cities
as I plucked you out of the desert
my rose dressed in wind and rain,
the two of us in the skiff
and my mad rebel slave's blood howling
howling till we reach the other shore.

VII

Nous deux dans la barque
et bleu de rancune l'océan alentour
les noyées remontent vers nous
pendues aux algues ;
Leurs yeux ne sont pas plus creux
leurs mains ne sont pas plus vides
que le cœur d'une ville...
N'est pas moins mortel le phare
                    qui nous guide.
Je mourrai de trop t'aimer ma rose
je mourrai d'être simplement une mère
mais que ma mort survienne
                    sur l'autre rive.

VII

The two of us in the skiff
and the ocean around us blue with spite
drowned women float up toward us
hanging from seaweed;
Their eyes are not hollower
their hands are not emptier
than the heart of a city . . .
No less deadly is the lighthouse
                    which guides us.
I will die of loving you too much, my rose
I will die from being simply a mother
but let that death happen
                    on the other shore.

VIII

Tourne-toi ma rose
regarde la ville
ses lumières tremblent
et son feu est éteint,
qui enterrera la ville ?
Quelle autre moitié de la mort
se lèvera pour rebâtir la ville ?
Quels poètes blessés
quels hommes lucides
iront à nouveau, au nouveau bûcher ?
Tourne-toi et regarde la ville :
Y vois-tu un arbre
une fleur
un oiseau ?
Y vois-tu un homme
une femme
qui soient encore debout ?
Puis regarde autour de toi la mort
                              crêtée
qui navigue
ma barque se remplit d'azur
nous mourrons de l'avoir voulue
                       nôtre
                          la ville.

VIII

Turn around my rose
look at the city
its lights are flickering
and its fire is put out,
who will bury the city?
What other half of death
will rise to rebuild the city?
What wounded poets
what clear-sighted men
will go again toward the new stake for burning?
Turn around and look at the city:
do you see a tree there
a flower
a bird?
Do you see a man there
or a woman
still standing?
Then look at that crested death
sailing
around you
my skiff fills up with azure
we will die for having wished
                         the city
                              ours.

IX

Toi qui me regardes m'en aller
et qui pleures
Toi qui m'offres tes allumettes
et tes baisers
qui m'offres tes eaux de noyé
Toi qui ne sais pas
et qui retiens ma barque
Toi avec ton poitrail
ta tendresse
ton sourire
Toi tout entier beau comme sait l'être
un homme pétri de soleil et de forêts
Tout entier toi
immobile sur les galets
et sanglotant sur le cadavre
                          que je serai
Toi et ton amour tous deux silencieux
et toujours pareils à vous-mêmes
sur votre rive
Toi qui savais toujours où ton amour
                          allait,
tu restes aujourd'hui sur ton roc
aussi pétrifié que lui
et moi dans ma barque
jusqu'au cou
glacée d'amour
ne voulant plus d'amour,
je ferme les yeux sur toi tout entier

IX

You who watch me leave
and weep
You who offer me your matches
and kisses
who offer me your drowned man's eyes
You who don't know
and who hold my skiff back
You with your broad chest
your tenderness
your smile
You entirely you handsome as only
a man molded by sun and forest knows how to be
Entirely you
motionless on the stone beach
and sobbing over the corpse
                    I will become
You and your love both silent
and always entirely yourselves
on your shore
You who knew always where your love
                              was going,
today you stay on your rock
as petrified as it is
and I in my skiff
frozen with love
up to my neck
wanting nothing more to do with love,
I close my eyes on you

debout
immobile parmi les mouettes,
toi que j'aimais si fort
que mon cœur de toutes ses jointures
a craqué.

entirely you
standing
motionless among the gulls,
you whom I loved so much
that my heart at every joint
               cracked open.

X

Je t'aimais
je ne te vois plus.
Ton amour ressemble à l'autre bout du monde
où quand j'arrive
j'ai peur de tomber de l'autre côté
                                    de la terre
j'ai peur de voir la terre d'en bas
j'ai peur de voir l'autre côté du ciel
ton amour y prend les proportions de l'enfer.
Ton amour est un ciel où je me perds
un ciel où tout s'arrête
jusqu'aux étoiles
jusqu'au soleil
jusqu'à la lune,
tout devient glace
devient piège
devient oiseau de proie
pour une mêlée de becs.
Je t'aimais, je ne te vois plus...
Avance ma barque.

X

I loved you
I no longer see you.
Your love seems like the other end of the world
where when I arrive
I'm afraid of falling off the other side
$\qquad\qquad\qquad$ *of the earth*
I'm afraid of seeing the earth from below
I'm afraid of seeing the other side of the sky
there your love seems to be as vast as hell.
Your love is a sky where I lose myself
a sky where everything stops
even the stars
even the moon
everything becomes ice
becomes a trap
becomes a bird of prey
in a carnage of beaks.
I loved you, I no longer see you . . .
Onward, my skiff.

XI

Je me délivre de la ville
et je vais où va l'eau.
Avec combien de larmes dans leur poitrine
                              contenues
combien de femmes ne sont-elles pas venues
remplir ton bassin
                    mer des vaincues ?
Porte ma barque aussi loin que tu peux
                              océan,
pour une fois que tu portes autre chose
                    que des épaves.
Porte ma barque
mon corps est beau
mon désir est grand
il jaillit de toi barque
              échappée à quelle eau...
Je est libre
et je déferle sur ses rives,
Je est libre
et déjà vague et déjà feu,
Je est libre
et j'avale tes récifs
océan des suicidées.

XI

I rescue myself from the city
and I go where the water goes.
With what weight of tears borne
                    in their chests
have how many women come
to refill your basin
            sea of vanquished women?
Carry my skiff as far as you can,
                    ocean,
for once you will be carrying something
                    besides flotsam.
Carry my skiff
my body is beautiful
my desire great
it bursts forth from you, skiff
                    escaped from what waters . . .
I is free
and I flow onto its banks,
I is free
already wave, already fire
I is free
and I swallow up your reefs
ocean of suicides.

XII

La nuit descend sur l'océan
et les noyés nous guident...
Combien êtes-vous morts pour
avoir rêvé d'une autre rive
d'une autre aube
d'une autre justice ?
Je te vois :
tu es une torche
dans ma nuit de femme
frère piégé
frère démoli
citoyen des villes souterraines
qui salue ma barque derrière tes barreaux.

Regarde-nous
depuis combien de temps allons-nous ainsi
les yeux serrés dans ce mouchoir ?
Combien de mouchoirs pour étouffer ta bouche ?
Combien d'autres bouches pour
pousser le même cri ?

Regarde
sur le mur ta main fait des traits
ta main compte les jours qui
                    nous séparent de l'Aube,
ton crayon est chaque jour plus petit.
Dis d'où viendra le cri ?

XII

Night falls on the ocean
and drowned men guide us . . .
How many of you died for
having dreamed of another shore
of another dawn
another justice?
I see you:
you are a torch
in my woman's night
trapped brother
ruined brother
citizen of underground cities
who hails my skiff from behind your bars.

Look at us
how long have we been going along like this
our eyes bound by this handkerchief?
How many handkerchiefs to smother your mouth?
How many other mouths to
raise the same cry?

Look
your hand is drawing lines on the wall
your hand counts the days which
                              separate us from the Dawn,
your pencil grows smaller every day.
Tell me, where does that cry come from?

La peur comme la mort est la fin
de toute chose...
Dis d'où viendra le cri ?

Fear, like death, is the end
of everything . . .
Tell me, where does that cry come from?

XIII

Et toi
toi l'ombre de toi-même
toi qui avances comme un cheval
la tête d'un côté et le corps de l'autre,
qui vois la moitié de la mer
et ne cesses de chercher l'autre,
qui mets tes yeux dans ta bouche
ta bouche dans une bouteille
la bouteille à la mer
et la mer entière dans une cigarette.
Toi assis sur un rocher la mer entière
roulant en fumée
dans ta poitrine.
Toi devenu cheval marin pour un soir
                              pour une nuit,
devenu cheval marin pour qu'il n'y ait
                              plus de nuit
pour qu'il n'y ait plus de matins
                              à te demander
sur quelle pierre déposer ta tête,
dans quelle poussière mettre ton pied
et plus d'autres matins à te demander
« Et aujourd'hui... ? »
Toi sur ton rocher
sans plus d'herbe à fumer
et pleurant l'océan perdu
et raclant de tes ongles un fond
                              de coquillage

XIII

And you
you the shadow of yourself
you who move forward like a horse
head on one side and body on the other,
who see one half of the sea
and don't stop searching for the other,
who put your eyes in your mouth
your mouth in a bottle
the bottle in the sea
and the whole sea in a cigarette.
You seated on a rock, the whole sea
rolling in smoke
into your chest.
You become sea horse for an evening
                    for a night,
become sea horse so that there will be

                    no more night
so that there will be no more mornings

                    to ask yourself

on what rock to rest your head,
in what dust to place your feet
and no other mornings to ask yourself
"And today . . . ?"
You on your rock
with no more grass to smoke
and crying for a lost ocean
and scraping a shard of seashell
                    with your nails

pour y trouver une parcelle de bruit.
Toi soudain redevenu fragile
redevenu homme
redevenu le pauvre que tu étais
avec tes souvenirs d'orphelinats
avec tes provisions de mégots
écoute ce que dit ma bouche.

to find a scrap of noise in it.
You suddenly become fragile again
a man again
become the pauper you used to be
with your memories of orphanages
with your stock of cigarette butts
listen to what my mouth pronounces.

XIV

La mer est à nous
la mer est à boire
la mer tout entière se loge
dans le creux de la main.
Si tu te remplissais
te barbouillais d'azur ?
Si ton pied foulait la mer ?
Si ta main apprenait les caresses océaniques ?
Si les vagues sur ton corps ?
Si les algues mêlées à ton désir ?
Si le sel sur tes blessures ?
Si la fureur de l'océan dans ton sang ?
Si soudain tu renaissais ?
Si soudain le rire ?
Soudain l'été ?
Soudain les plages de ton enfance et
                              les chansons ?
Si soudain tu voyais des deux yeux ?
Si tu entendais des deux oreilles
le cri de toutes les bouches ?
Et si soudain tu te levais ?
Et si tout aussi soudain tu te mettais
                              à dire Non ?

XIV

The sea is ours
the sea is there to drink
all the sea is cupped
in the palm of your hand.
If you filled yourself up
daubed yourself with azure?
If your feet tread on the sea?
If your hands learned oceanic caresses?
If the waves on your body?
If seaweed tangled in your desire?
If the salt on your wounds?
If the ocean's rage in your blood?
If suddenly you were reborn?
If suddenly laughter?
Suddenly summer?
Suddenly your childhood's beaches
                    and the songs?
If suddenly you saw with both eyes?
If you heard with both ears
the cry of all those mouths?
And if suddenly you arose?
And just as suddenly began
                    to say No?

XV

C'était un conte pour femmes défigurées
pour enfants sans rire.
Un conte-fracas dans le jardin de verre
après des siècles de rondes
des siècles de silence
dans le palais de Shahrayar.

Ce fut le conte-sanglot d'une femme déchirée
le conte-sanglant d'une tête tranchée
     sur le chemin de l'émeute...
Et sans une larme, dans le jardin de verre,
prit la relève, la chouette
     la plus noire.

XV

It was a tale for disfigured women
for children unable to laugh.
A tale crashing in the glass garden
after centuries of patrols
centuries of silence
in Shehriyar's palace.

It was the sobbing tale of a shattered woman
the bloody tale of a head severed

                    on the way to revolt . . .
And without a tear, in the glass garden,
the blackest owl

            took its turn to stand guard.

TROISIÈME CONTE

I

Vois cet amour entêté
à déchaîner araignées et poursuites
au plafond de l'oubli.

Seule
moi, femme d'ébène
cœur et corps aux cris noirs
à l'intérieur de coffres sans fonds
où l'enfer de mon prénom croasse,
où Émeraude je suis
mes flammes vertes
ma haine froide
et toute la cohorte de mes rêves
résumés dans un bout de papier
où je suis esclave affranchie
délivrée des cours et couronnes royales,
désormais libre pour me procurer un travail rémunéré
moyennant une soirée aux chandelles
dans le clandestin et l'anonymat,
pouvoir ainsi dans la soumission des feuilles blanches
et papier carbone,
jusqu'à l'érosion de mes ongles écarlates,
taper le savoir de mon nouveau maître
patron et seigneur
les rendez-vous de la mort,
les dîners d'affaires où
à l'éternelle-épouse-absente se substitue

THIRD TALE

I

See this love determined
to turn loose spiders and prosecutions
on the ceiling of oblivion.
Alone
I, woman of ebony
my heart's and my body's black clamor
inside bottomless coffers
where the hell of my name caws,
where I am Emerald
my green flames
my cold hatred
and the whole horde of my dreams
summed up on a scrap of paper
where I am a freed slave
liberated from royal courts and crowns,
henceforth free to find paid work
for the price of a candlelit evening
clandestine and anonymous,
to be able, through white pages'
and carbon paper's submission,
to type my new master's knowledge
my boss and my lord
till my scarlet nails wear down
his assignations with death,
the business dinners where
the eternal-absent-wife is replaced

la lycéenne-adolescente-et-vierge.
Un Martini pour toi la môme
pour que les caresses soient moins furtives
et que dure l'amour le temps
que dure un jet de sperme
sur ta cuisse de gazelle,
ceintures d'or enserrant autour de tes hanches
l'étau des solitudes lunaires.
Moi
à jamais seule
et femme d'ébène
à vouloir traverser bulles
abcès
et barouds
pour dissiper les malentendus,
à vouloir trouver les mots justes
pour te situer mon corps
                    dans ce cloaque
mon corps déchiqueté
dans les dédales d'un conte maudit
dans un palais maudit
au cœur d'un pays pétrifié,
royaume de cloîtres et jardins intérieurs
où pousse luxuriante et baveuse
une flore carnivore à tige exacerbée
par les vidéos pornos
par les pétrodollars
par un soleil déclaré officiellement cause
de tous les désastres,

by the virgin-high-school-girl.
A Martini for you, kid,
so these caresses will be less furtive
and love will last as long
as a spurt of sperm
on your gazelle thigh,
golden sashes tightening on your hips
in a noose of lunar solitude.
I
alone forever
woman of ebony
who wished to cross bubbles
abscesses
and battles
to dissolve misunderstandings
who wished to find the right words
to locate my body for you
                    in this sewer
my tattered body
in the maze of an accursed story
in an accursed palace
at the heart of a petrified country,
kingdom of cloisters and walled gardens
where, dripping and luxuriant
carnivorous flora grow, stems lengthened
by porn videos
and petrodollars
by a sun declared the official cause
of all disasters,

depuis la sécheresse
le rationnement de l'eau, de la parole
du geste
jusqu'aux insolations-émeutes
qui déclenchent au-dessus des villes hurlantes
et prises au dépourvu
la férocité de nuées d'oiseaux carnassiers
semant à travers médinas terreur
et cadavres d'enfants
retournant voler ces mêmes cadavres
pour que l'Histoire
ah, l'Histoire...

Pays pétrifié où Shahrayar et djinns,
alliés en plein jour
pour l'oppression suprême,
acculent à se retrancher dans sa peur
son verre de thé
son Football
tout mon peuple d'affamés.

Comme Dinazarde nous avons été témoins
muettes et complices
                    de notre propre mort
du partage de notre corps en petites étoiles
hennissantes de plaisir
et en tête jetée aux chiens :
un os à ronger
et rien de plus.

from drought and
water-rationing to speech
movements
to sunstroke-riots,
which explode above howling cities
caught off-guard
the blood-lust of carnivorous birds in flocks
sowing terror
and children's corpses through the medinas
coming back to pillage those same corpses
so that History
ah, History . . .

Petrified country where Shehriyar and genies,
daylight allies
in total repression,
drives them back, to take refuge in fear
in cups of tea
in football,
my whole famished people.

Like Dinazarde we were witnesses
silent and complicit
                 of our own death
of our bodies' division into little stars
whinnying with pleasure
our heads thrown to the dogs:
another bone to gnaw
and nothing more.

Assez parlé autour de mon peuple
                              assassiné
aucune prière ne monte à mes lèvres,
aucune larme
puits tari
je craque de tous mes murs
de tous les siècles encaissés
et dynasties identiques.
Seule
et femme d'ébène
                    pour l'éternité
je suis la courbe des siècles crevés
pour trouver une eau limpide
où laver tes pieds,
                    Shahrazade,
avant d'enterrer tes mains couvertes de henné
bijoux compris et
                    chants sordides
                              des esclaves libérées.

Enough has been said about my murdered
                              people

no prayer rises to my lips
no tear
dry well
all my walls crack open
from all the hoarded centuries
and identical dynasties.
Alone
and woman of ebony
                  eternally
I am the curve of centuries pierced
in search of clear water
with which to wash your feet,
                        Scheherazade,
before burying your henna-covered hands
their jewels with them and
                    their squalid songs
                              of freed slaves.

II

Ah, combien elle a rêvé d'océans nocturnes
remontant la saveur du sel et du sang

                    dans nos gorges

rêvé
comme si elle connaissait tous les mots
à combiner
pour qu'une porte s'ouvre
qu'un peuple se redresse
et qu'enfin la mer déferle

         dans nos têtes-brasiers

où il y a si peu de place pour qu'une femme
continue à hurler
une porte à se fermer sur un homme
qu'on torture
un enfant qu'on sodomise
rêvé
de toutes les mers en furie
comme si un continent rouge allait surgir
au milieu des mers
comme si ce continent pouvait allumer

                    tous les miroirs

ces carrés de détresse
ces lacs
et tordre à jamais son cou
au serpent pelé de la mort
le Sultan-Furoncle
visiblement reptile et séduisant
— des siècles de séduction et de ruses tissés

II

How often she dreamed of nocturnal oceans
bringing the taste of blood and salt
                  back up in our throats
dreamed
as if she knew all the words
to put together
so that a door would open
a people arise
and the sea finally flood
               into our heads' lit coals
where there is so little space that a woman
would keep screaming
a door keep closing on a man
being tortured
a boy being raped
she dreamed
of all the seas enraged
as if a red continent would thrust up
amidst the seas
as if this continent could light up
               all the mirrors
those squares of sorrow
those lakes
and once and for all wring the neck
of the mangy serpent of death
the Sultan of Abscesses
reptilian and seductive
—centuries of seduction and woven ruses

dans sa tête triangulaire

      et subtile

         et meurtrière —

Ah, combien elle a rêvé d'océans nocturnes
pour se jeter finalement dans

      cet infini définitif

         du Non,

le pays d'avant la mort
l'aridité absolue

      des espaces livides.

in his triangular
      subtle
           and murderous head—

How often she dreamed of nocturnal oceans
to throw herself at last in
           that final infinity
               of No,
the country before death
the absolute dryness
           of white spaces.

III

Finis, engloutis par les égouts du réel
mes départs vers des continents vierges
de toute trace de patriarche,
mes projets absurdes vers le large
où je suis maîtresse des mers
de moi-même et des navires
                                en perdition.

J'ai noyé mes rêves océaniques
où j'étais sirène
— vision de cauchemar insinuée dans mon sommeil
par Sindbad, le loup des mers —
un fantasme d'homme
pour me séparer de moi-même,
toujours ou nier la tête
                ou trafiquer le corps...

Il n'y a pas de mer ni d'île
où je puis être
sans cette marée de nausée à être
autrement que située
mutilée
par une parole d'homme
précédant mon désir de naître.

Il n'y a pas de mer où je puis me laver
de mille et une nuits
contes vagins-à-ogives.

III

Done with, swallowed by the sewers of reality
my departures toward continents innocent
of any patriarch's touch
my preposterous aspirations toward the open
where I am mistress of the seas
of myself of lost
            ships.

I have drowned my oceanic dreams
where I was a mermaid
—nightmare vision insinuated into my sleep
by Sinbad, the sea-wolf—
a fantasy man,
to separate me from myself,
always either denying the head
            or trafficking the body . . .

There is neither sea nor island
where I can exist
without that tide of nausea at being
something not located
mutilated
by a man's word
that came before my desire to be born.

There is no sea where I can wash myself
of the thousand and one nights'
vaulted vagina-tales.

Il n'y a qu'une terre gangrenée
sans eau
sans sommeil
sans pardon.
Une terre de violence
où je ne garde des sirènes que les écailles
pour m'allier au serpent originel
et te déloger, Shahrayar
de ma peau de femme.

There is only a gangrenous land
without water
sleep
or pardon.
A violent land
where all I keep of mermaids is their scales
to ally myself with the first serpent
and evict you, Shehriyar,
from my woman's skin.

IV

Il retourne sur les lieux du crime
le chameau dont je porte
la bosse.
Il me tutoie
parle du beau temps
il rit d'être chameau
de n'avoir jamais soif
d'être le seul à pouvoir
me livrer la clé des étendues mortes
il prend le turban du sage...
Il prend feu dans ma poitrine
le chameau
dont je porte la bosse.

IV

He comes back to the scene of the crime
the camel
whose hump I bear.
He speaks to me familiarly
talks of the fine weather
he laughs about being a camel
and never thirsty
being the only one who can
give me the key to the dead deserts
he puts on the wise man's turban . . .
he flames up in my breast
the camel
whose hump I bear.

V

Je soulève le premier voile
et ouvre la première porte
où l'enfer premier est un enfer de mots.
Des caravanes s'ébranlent en moi
et descendent vers des contrées désertiques
où nul chien n'aboie
où nul insecte ne bouge.
Du Nord au Sud des crânes
comme seuls compagnons de route...
Ils se taisent
et je m'entends parler de paix
avec des poèmes
                    de guerre...

V

I lift the first veil
and open the first door
where the first hell is a hell of words.
Caravans set off within me
and descend toward desert lands
where no dog barks
no insect budges.
From North to South skulls
are my only traveling companions . . .
They keep still
and I hear myself speak of peace
with poems
          of war . . .

VI

Vers quel lambeau d'horizon jaune
cette femme partie
comme celui qui s'éveille
voit une porte s'ouvrir en lui
mais qui crie
parce qu'elle s'ouvre sur un gouffre
et qu'il chevauche un chameau aveugle ?

Comme cette eau enfuie de sa bouche, partie
qui laisse gerçures et crevasses
mots gelés
mots épines
mots revanche
libérant dans la gorge
le chant des détresses muettes.
Partie
comme une pierre lancée
                    pour meurtrir
les rêves falsifiés
qui ricochent sur le vide
et retournent briser les dents.

Vers quelle bataille ?
Avec quelle arme partie ?
Quelle quantité de paille
pour maintenir le feu allumé
dans la bouche ?

VI

Toward what rag of yellow horizon
has this woman gone
like the man who wakes
sees a door open within him
but who cries out
because it opens on an abyss
and he rides a blind camel?

Like that water spilled from her mouth, gone,
leaving cracks and fissures
frozen words
thorny words
vengeful words
freeing in her throat
the song of silent anguish.
Gone
like a stone thrown
                    to bruise
counterfeit dreams
that ricochet over the void
and return to break your teeth.

Toward what battle?
Gone with what arms?
How much straw
to keep the fire in
her mouth alight?

VII

Par quelle déchirure
voie de violence et de sang
tu es entrée
Soif
dans ce corps sans ombre ?
Vite une oasis
un puits
une trêve.
La mort le rire aux côtes
le rire aux griffes
lance ses vautours
sur mes épaules nues.
Si je tombe le soleil frappe
et des serpents de routes m'assaillent
et dévoient mes caravanes.
Si je tente vers le ciel
un cri de rage et d'agonie
mon appel se perd
            dans le silence
toujours plus fort
            que la tempête.
Mais allié au piège des sables mouvants
mon cri rend impracticable
le chemin de l'oubli.

VII

Through what rip
what trail of blood and violence
did you enter
Thirst
in this body with no shadow?
Quick an oasis
a well
a truce.
Death with laughter swelling its ribs
laughter in its claws
sets its vultures
at my naked shoulders.
If I fall the sun strikes
and the snakes of the road will attack me
and lead my caravans astray.
If I attempt to cry
my rage and pain to the heavens
my call is lost
                in a silence
always stronger
                than the storm.
But linked to the snare of shifting sands
my cry bars the way to
the path of oblivion.

VIII

Ce n'est pas un appel
pour recueillir la pluie
ni pour crever les citernes
ni pour creuser un puits
pas même pour rester stoïque
comme une sentinelle au bord du gel.
C'est un acte pour résumer les mots
dans la bouche
comme le tonnerre résume la colère
des cieux.
Après le cri elle se tait
plus fort
pour en mesurer la portée aux échos
des grottes.
Elle se tait pour souffler
dans les canons vides
soupeser les sacs de poudre
et rajuster son tir.

VIII

This is not a plea
to collect rainwater
nor to burst the cisterns
nor to dig a well
not even to stay stoic
as a watchman beside the ice.
It's an act to sum up words
in a mouth
as thunder sums up the rage
of the skies.
After the cry she is even
more silent
to measure its reach against
the grotto's echoes.
She is silent so she can breathe
in the empty cannons
lift and weigh the sacks of gunpowder
and take aim.

IX

L'oiseau qui parle dans les montagnes
à combien de cimes de sagesse
à partir de ma plume ?
À quelle distance de moi ?
À quelle hauteur de femme
dressée dans la colère
pour que je puisse mesurer
la chute de l'eau dans ma gorge où soif
soif
comme si le ciel n'existait
que pour étendre cet infini de plages
d'ossements
entre toi et moi
                    femme ?

IX

The bird that speaks in the mountains
at how many peaks of wisdom
from my own pen?
At what distance from me?
From what woman's height
erect in her anger
so that I can measure
the water pouring in my throat where thirst
thirst
as if the sky only existed
to extend the infinity of bone-
strewn beaches
between us

      woman?

X

Elle s'est barricadée car elle sait
combien le désert est traître.
Elle en fait un sablier
et fixe son cou à la chute
du dernier grain de cristal.
En attendant elle place une mine
dans chaque poème qu'elle lance
sans savoir quel front il ira ruiner
avant que dans sa bouche
la parole lui soit reprise.

X

She has barricaded herself for she knows
how the desert betrays.
She makes an hourglass of it
and lays her neck where the last
crystal grain will fall.
Waiting, she places a mine
into each poem she launches
without knowing what forehead it will burst
before the word
in her mouth is taken back from her.

XI

Aller jusqu'au bout de l'effritement
et perdre la paix des pierres muettes
à force de sable.

Quand la parole préméditée
perpétue le chant des cascades
jusque dans cette eau de vaisselle
à la bouche des égouts
à quelle porte frapper
pour en avertir les naïades ?

Dans quel champ brûlé à l'avance
mes mots iront tomber en convulsions
sans que rien ne frémisse
dans celui qui écoute
sans que rien ne s'arrête
dans moi qui parle
qui marche
et m'agrandis
d'un désert de plus ?

XI

To go just to the edge of erosion
and lose the mute stones' peace
having crumbled into sand.

When the forethought word
carries the waterfalls' singing
as far as this dishwater
bubbling in the drain
at what door should we knock
to warn the naiads?

In what already burned field
will my words convulse
while not a muscle trembles
in the one who listens
or in me, speaking
moving forward
and growing
in one more desert?

XII

Le temps passe et lui emporte la moitié
du visage
tandis que dans l'autre
il lui reste si peu de mots
si peu d'images
qu'elle n'arrive même pas à faire
un livre de pauvre.
Si peu de salive qu'à racler l'aride
sa voix sèche et se brise.

Perdu le rêve des mers hurlantes
montant à l'assaut des palais de jade,
perdu par le sortilège des souhaits de
longue vie et de prospérité
pour Shahrayar.

Elle ne peut plus se lancer sur la trace
des renégats
elle ne peut plus avancer
elle ne peut plus dire si sela fait mal.
Elle ne sait plus si elle écrit à tâtons
où si les mots se jettent à sa face
elle ne sait plus avec quel bâton fouiller
quel espace.
Elle écrit en aveugle
et la peur l'accompagne.

XII

Time passes and takes away
half her face
while the other keeps
so few words
so few images
that she can not even write
a pauper's book.
So little saliva that her voice
dries out and breaks
on arid scraping.
Lost now, the dream of howling seas
that besieged the jade palace,
lost through the spell of wishing
long life and wealth
to Shehriyar.
She can no longer set off
following the renegades
she can no longer move forward
she can not say if this hurts her.
She no longer knows if she gropes forward by writing
or if words hurl themselves in her face
she no longer knows with what staff to dig into
what space.
She writes blindly
and fear goes with her.

XIII

Se taire n'est pas juste.

Jusqu'où m'enfoncer dans le désert
pour écrire plus nu
plus simple
plus loin ?
Quand je ne verrai plus mes caravanes
quand tout sera feu sur mon passage
quand je serai détachée
rassasiée d'orages
quand le désert l'emportera,
je m'essayerai sur une dune
et récrirai les mille et une nuits
pour réhabiliter Shahrazade.

XIII

To remain silent is unjust.
Where to disappear in the desert
to write more nakedly
more simply
farther?
When I can no longer see my caravans
when fire has erased my passage
when I am detached
have had my fill of storms
when the desert carries everything away
I will climb onto a dune
and rewrite the thousand and one nights
to clear Scheherazade's name.

XIV

Ainsi le gouffre sera plus grand
cris de loups dans
     les gerçures de l'amour.
Tu as bien fait de jeter des
      plages de silences
dans les discours susurrés
      au clair de lune,
j'ai bien fait de planter des barbelés
entre toi et moi
mais je ne sais comment des poèmes
éclaboussés de ton sang
sont venus un à un
    se ficher en moi.

Il est vrai que le vent aggrave
      les solitudes
qu'aux cimes des dunes se hissent
      les nostalgies
et qu'il pousse des champs d'amour
au milieu des orties.
Mais il me coûte de te héler
à coups d'écrits amers
où la colère l'emporte et m'apparente
      à l'ouragan,
de te perdre entre les lignes
qui t'infligent le spectacle de
      mes entailles
tes ruines et mes défaites.

XIV

So the gulf will be wider
wolves' howling in
                    love's fissures.
Just as well that you cast
                    layers of silence
into the speeches whispered
                    in the moonlight,
just as well that I stretched barbed wire
between you and me
but I don't know how these poems
splattered with your blood
have come one by one
                    to pierce me.

It is true that the wind increases
                    solitudes
that nostalgia hoists itself up
                    to the dune's peak
and that fields of love grow
in the midst of nettles.
But it hurts me to call to you
with embittered writing
where anger takes over and makes me sister
                    to a hurricane,
to lose you between the lines
that inflict on you the sight of
                    my gashed skin
your ruins and my defeats.

Il me coûte de nous retrouver
à couteaux tirés dans les artères
de cette ville
> *déjà lointaine*
où je suis
à force de nous déchirer
le plus rien sans porte
> *des recommencements.*
Mais c'est désormais ma façon d'être
je n'ai pas à t'épargner
dans la cohue des souks
en proie à la démence
dans la foudre des vérités
> *enfin crachées.*
Je n'ai pas à t'épargner
nous nous aimerons plus tard...
Beaucoup plus tard
dans les cendres
> *des palais de cristal.*

It hurts me to find us
with knives drawn in the arteries
of this already
         distant city
where rending us apart
has left me
out of reach of
         new beginnings.
But this is my way from now on.
I need not spare you
in the clamor of the marketplace
prey to madness
in the thunder of truths
         spat out at last.
I do not need to spare you
we will love each other later . . .
Much later
in the ashes
         of the crystal palaces.

XV

Hivers autour de ses rides
à mesure que le temps passe
s'installe blanc
en couches de poudres épaisses
                                de mutisme,
inaudible elle demeure.
Encore un conte qui s'allonge
                                et se rétracte
en nœuds vissés à sa gorge
en verrous aux portes profondes
en vœux inaccessibles
                        à son pied infirme,
illisible elle demeure.

Illisible d'une seule main
tandis que de l'autre
sur pages blanches et
                        terres inconnues
elle déchaîne la horde de ses fantasmes :
vagues brisées
chergui, agonie et meurtre...
car tu es ce loup
— le dernier de son espèce —
qui sème encore panique et lèpre
dans le troupeau de ses rêves
et parle d'amour au clair de lune.

XV

Winters gather around her wrinkles
as time passes
and installs itself colorless
in thick powdery layers
                    of silence,
she is still unheard.
Here is another story that lengthens
                    and shrinks
in knots screwed into her throat
in bolts on the heaviest doors
in wishes her crippled feet
                    cannot reach,
she is still unread.

Unread by one hand
while with the other
on white pages and
                    unknown territories
she sets free her fantasy horde:
waves breaking
sirocco, death and murder . . .
for you are that wolf
—the last of the species—
who still sows plague and panic
among the flock of her dreams
and speaks of love in the moonlight.

C'est pourquoi de ses ongles
elle laboure des nuits entières
pour que mise à nu la lune
dans la nuit la plus labourée
n'abrite plus que des
                          amours mortes.

C'est pourquoi le front au mur
elle balance aux pendules des douleurs
et du pied elle fouille
                    le vide.

C'est pourquoi à l'aube des désastres
au crissement des premières rides
pour naître femme
elle en est encore à puiser dans l'amour
                                        et les larmes
les contes
          où elle manque
                          ses armes.

Hivers
hivers autour de mes rides.
Une fumée m'emplit la poitrine
à mesure que je parle...
Est-ce déjà le feu qui s'allume
                        dans les palais de cristal ?
Est-ce déjà mon feu qui s'allume
                        dans l'auditoire ?

That is why she digs
nightlong with her bare nails
so that the moon, stripped naked
in the plow-furrowed darkness,
will shelter only
                    dead loves.

That is why, her head against the wall,
she swings from the pendulum of sorrows
and probes the void
                    with her foot.

That is why, at the dawn of disasters
at the rustling of her first wrinkles
having been born a woman,
she keeps drawing from love
                                and tears
those stories
            where she is without
                                    her weapons.

Winters
winters gathered around my wrinkles.
Smoke fills my throat
as I speak . . .
Is it the fire being lit even now
*   in the crystal palaces?*
Is it the fire flaming up even now
*   among my listeners?*

Est-ce déjà mon feu

        le feu qui vous anime ?

Certitude d'incendies
sang et baroud...
Brûle comme je flambe
brûle de toutes les branches

        de tes amandiers en fleurs
comme je m'embrase de tous les enfers
de mes prénoms de femme

        brûle
ô terre brûlante de mes ancêtres

        barbares et rancuniers...

            et que conte

              s'ensuive.

Is it my fire now
　　　the fire that brings you to life?

Certainty of fires
blood and battles . . .
Burn as I flame
burn from all the branches
　　　　of your flowering almond trees
burn as I blaze from all my hells
of women's names,

　　　　　burn
O burning earth of my barbarous
　　　　and vengeful ancestors . . .

　　　　　　and let a story
　　　　　　　　emerge.

CREDITS

"I am there": "Je suis là," from Rachida Madani, *Femme je suis*, in Madani, *Blessures au vent* (Paris: Éditions de la Différence, 2006)

Sections of these sequences have appeared in

Asymptote (asymptotejournal.com): "The Second Tale," VI, VII, IX, XIII

Banipal: A Journal of Modern Arab Literature (UK): "The Second Tale," I–V

Callalloo (US): "The Third Tale," I, II

Magma (UK): "The First Tale," I, II, IV, VII, X, XXV

Modern Poetry in Translation (UK): "The Third Tale," I–IX

Poetry Review (UK): "The Third Tale," X, XII, XIV

Women's Studies Quarterly (US): "The First Tale," complete, acknowledging previous publications

WordsWithoutBorders (wordswithoutborders.org): "The First Tale," I, II, IV, VII, VIII, IX, X, XII, XXIII, XXV

Language for a New Century: Contemporary Poetry from the Middle East, Asia, and Beyond, ed. Tina Chang, Nathalie Handal, and Ravi Shankar (New York: Norton, 2008): "The First Tale," I